# Arthur and the Race to Read

**A Marc Brown** **Chapter Book**

# Arthur and the Race to Read

Text by Stephen Krensky

## Little, Brown and Company

Boston    New York    London

First Edition

The characters and events portrayed in this book are fictitious. Any
similarity to real persons, living or dead, is coincidental and not intended
by the author.

Arthur® is a registered trademark of Marc Brown.

Text has been reviewed and assigned a reading level by Laurel S. Ernst,
M.A., Teachers College, Columbia University, New York, New York;
reading specialist, Chappaqua, New York

ISBN 0-316-11816-8 (hc) — 0-316-12024-3 (pb)
Library of Congress Control Number 00-106831

HC: 10 9 8 7 6 5 4 3 2 1
PB: 10 9 8 7 6 5 4 3 2 1

WOR (hc)
COM-MO (pb)

Printed in the United States of America

For my friend and collaborator,
Steve Krensky
— M. B.

# Chapter 1

● ● ● ● ● ● ● ● ● ●

Arthur thought his chest was going to explode.

His third-grade class was racing around the track during gym. Miss Grimslid, the gym teacher, had the students running in pairs, and they were supposed to stay together. Arthur was trying to keep up with Sue Ellen, but it wasn't easy.

"Come on, Arthur," she said. "Feel the burn!"

"I-I'm feeling all kinds of things," Arthur gasped. "Burning, stabbing pains, aches . . ."

Sue Ellen shook her head. "You've got to be tough, Arthur. It's important to stay in shape. I try to run almost every day. It makes me faster. And I feel better, too."

Arthur sighed. "The only time I run fast is when I'm chasing D.W." He paused. "Or when D.W. is chasing me."

A short distance behind them, Francine and Buster were running together.

"Step it up, Buster," said Francine. "We don't want Sue Ellen and Arthur to get all the glory."

"There's glory here?" Buster said.

Francine nodded. "Fame and fortune are always waiting just around the corner. Now, come on. It's time to make our move."

Another few yards back, the Brain and Muffy were shuffling along.

"I think we're falling behind," said Muffy.

"Nonsense," said the Brain. "Our plan is working perfectly."

Muffy looked surprised. "We have a plan?" she said. "I didn't know that."

"It's a question of draft and wind resistance," the Brain explained. "Here in the middle of the pack, we benefit from the airflow of the runners in front of us. We're sucked along by the draft they create."

"Will that help us win?"

The Brain laughed. "Win? I'm not trying to win. I'm just hoping to survive."

Muffy glanced behind them. "Well, at least we're not last."

This was true. Fern and Binky were bringing up the rear. Their pace was steady, but Binky looked frustrated.

"Fern, I know I'm supposed to be your partner, but can't we go faster?"

"Why?"

"Because we're behind everyone else." Binky frowned. "I hate that."

"Speed isn't everything," said Fern. "We can appreciate the sun on our faces and the greenness of the grass. We're setting a good pace."

"If it's so good, how come we're in last place?"

"Everybody's different, Binky," said Fern. "Our pace is good for us. It doesn't have to be good for anybody else."

"Well, maybe you should—," Binky started.

"Just relax and enjoy the view," said Fern.

Binky looked around. "What view? This is gym class."

"Use your imagination. Anyway, we're not doing so bad. Arthur and Sue Ellen are behind us. But don't be too obvious when you look. We don't want to embarrass them."

Binky groaned. "They're not behind us, Fern."

"They're not?"

"They're so far ahead of us that we're

5

going to be lapped! Can't you go any faster?"

Fern shook her head. She didn't know how many speeds she had, but she knew that none of them were any faster than the speed she was going now.

Arthur and Sue Ellen were getting closer . . . and closer.

"They're going to catch us for sure!" moaned Binky.

And then Miss Grimslid blew the whistle.

"Saved by the bell," said Binky. For once he was happy gym was over.

# Chapter 2

• • • • • • • • • • • •

"All right, everyone, settle down," said Mr. Ratburn, as the class returned from gym. "Before we get started with math, I want to tell you about an upcoming event. As you may know, a lot of children do not have enough opportunities to read and learn about reading. Lakewood Elementary is sponsoring a literacy drive to help them out, and we're all going to participate as part of a class project."

"How will the money be raised?" asked the Brain.

"There's going to be a race," Mr. Ratburn explained. "You will get sponsors to pledge money in support of your running. However, this will not be a contest to see who can raise the most money. Any and all donations are welcome. The race, though, will be competitive. The whole school will run together, but there will be one winner from each grade. So you won't be competing against anyone older — or younger — than yourself. And each winner will get a special prize. Any questions?"

"If we raise more money, do we get a head start?" Muffy asked.

"Sorry. Everyone will start in the same place at the same time."

Fern raised her hand. "Do we have to run? I mean, couldn't we help out in another way?"

Mr. Ratburn shook his head. "Everyone is to participate, Fern. No exceptions. The race is not till next week, though, so you'll all have time to prepare. With a little work, you'll be ready to face anyone, even a messenger like Phidippides, one of the most famous runners in history. Have any of you heard of him?"

The Brain raised his hand. "In 490 B.C. there was a fierce battle at Marathon between the Greeks and the Persians. Phidippides supposedly ran over twenty-five miles to relay the news of the victory."

"That's a long way," said Muffy. "Did he get a reward?"

Mr. Ratburn shook his head. "Sadly, no. He collapsed and died after giving the news."

Everyone groaned.

"This only underscores the importance of training," said Mr. Ratburn. "Now the name 'Marathon' came down to us as a twenty-six-mile race. But we're not going to be running any marathons here. This will be a five-kilometer event. That's about

three miles. It will not take place on a track, but will wind through the town."

Arthur made a face.

"I got here as fast as I could," he said, gasping for breath.

He was standing at the steps of a marble building with tall pillars.

"You're too late!" said Prime Minister Brain, folding his arms.

"I kept tripping over my toga," Arthur explained. "That really slowed me down."

"I am not interested in your excuses, and the empress won't be, either."

"The empress?" Arthur gasped. "She's here?"

Prime Minister Brain stepped aside.

"You're late," said Empress Francine, sitting on her throne.

"But I did my best. And none of the roads are paved. And there were wolves chasing me!"

The empress waved him to silence. "That

should only have made you run faster." She turned to her guards. "Take him away!"

"No!" Arthur wailed. But his cries were ignored as he was dragged off to the dungeon.

# Chapter 3

• • • • • • • • • • • •

After school, Arthur and his friends went to the Sugar Bowl. Arthur, Francine, Sue Ellen, and Buster sat in one booth. The Brain, Muffy, Binky, and Fern sat in another.

"Buster, you've been looking at the menu forever," said Francine. "Have you decided what to order?"

"Yup. The triple-scoop deluxe banana skyscraper supreme."

"Not a good idea," said the Brain, twisting around to face him. "You should start thinking about the race, Buster. All those extra calories will weigh you down."

"Don't worry," said Buster. "They'll be long gone before then." He turned to Arthur. "Are you all right? You look a little pale."

"You'd be pale, too, if you'd been cooped up in a smelly old dungeon."

"Huh?"

Arthur sighed. "Never mind."

Sue Ellen was writing in her notebook.

"What are you doing?" Binky asked.

"Working out an exercise schedule. Arthur and I have a lot of training to do."

"We do?" Arthur's eyes opened wide. "Why me?"

"We've already been paired up in gym. And training is lonely if you do it alone. It'll be more fun this way."

"That's a good idea," said Francine. "That means you're with me, Buster."

"And you're with me, Muffy," said the Brain.

Binky frowned. "And I'm with . . . Fern," he said.

But Fern didn't seem to be listening. "It's terrible," she said, "to think there are children who don't get a good chance to learn to read."

"Yeah," said Buster, "that must be tough. They never know which ice-cream flavor is the daily special."

"Or what the score is at a ball game," Binky added.

"There are more important reasons than that," said Fern. "Literature, and poetry, and —"

"But let's not forget the main thing," said Francine. "Which is winning the race."

"I wonder what the special prize is," said Muffy.

Francine shrugged. "There's nothing more special than a bicycle."

Sue Ellen shook her head. "Francine, I

don't think anyone would give a bicycle as a prize in a *running* race."

"Well, they should."

"Why is that?"

"Because I want a new bicycle, that's why. And I plan to win."

"Well, what if I win?" said Buster. "I don't need a new bicycle. A baseball glove would be better."

"Or a skateboard," said Binky.

"Winning the race will not be easy," the Brain reminded them.

"Sure it will," said Francine. "All I have to do is beat everyone else."

"True," said the Brain, "but how will you beat them? That's the question. There will be issues of weather, the terrain . . ."

"Don't forget being in great shape," said Sue Ellen.

"Wouldn't good shape be enough?" asked Arthur. "Or even pretty good shape?"

"You have to have the right stride. . . ."

"And plant your foot right."

"And breathe in just before you breathe out."

Fern looked back and forth from one head to another. She was getting a headache. As everyone kept talking, she quietly got up and left.

No one even noticed.

# Chapter 4

. . . . . . . . . . . .

That night at dinner, Arthur finished his chicken first. Then he lined up a few peas in a row next to his mashed potatoes. He poked each pea with his fork to see how far forward it rolled.

"What are you doing?" asked D.W.

"Um, nothing."

"It looks like you're racing your peas."

"Don't be silly, D.W. Why would anyone race peas?"

D.W. stopped to think. "I don't know. Oh, wait, yes I do. It's that racing thing I heard you talking to Buster about."

"Racing thing?" said Mr. Read. "What racing thing?"

"It has nothing to do with the peas," said Arthur. Then he told them all about the race.

"A literacy race?" said his mother. "That's certainly a worthy cause. It's an embarrassment in this day and age that so many children still don't get a proper chance to read."

D.W. frowned. "What kind of race will it be? Are you going to see who reads the fastest?"

"No, D.W. It's a race for reading, not a reading race. We get people to sponsor us, and then we run a regular race. The goal is to make people realize how important reading is, and to raise money at the same time. Mr. Ratburn says that reading is the hub on the Wheel of Learning."

D.W. frowned again. "What does that mean?"

"Well, I'm not exactly sure, but it sounds important."

"It means," said Mr. Read, "that no matter what you want to learn about, reading is in the middle of it. We'll be glad to sponsor you, Arthur. And I'll check with Grandma Thora and Grandpa Dave. I'm sure they'll want to chip in, too."

"Five kilometers is a pretty long way," said Mrs. Read. "When I ran track in high school, that was considered a cross-country distance."

"You were a runner?" said D.W.

Her mother nodded. "The two hundred meters and the four hundred meters. And it's a good thing, too. Otherwise, I'd never be able to keep up with you, D.W."

"Did you ever run a five k yourself?" Arthur asked.

"Not in competition," said his mother. "But if you're really going to run the whole way, you'll have to be in good shape."

Arthur sighed. "That's what Sue Ellen keeps saying. We're supposed to start practicing together."

"Sue Ellen is fast," said D.W. "You can't keep up with her."

"I can, too," Arthur insisted. "I just don't care as much about it as she does."

"There's a lot of strategy to running," said Mrs. Read. "You want to stay up with the leaders, but you don't want to get in front too soon. And you always want to save some energy for the final *kick* at the end."

"There's going to be one winner for each grade," said Arthur. "And a special prize, too."

"So, Arthur," said D.W., "who do you think will win?"

"Well, anyone has a chance, even me."

D.W. just laughed.

Arthur looked down at his plate and ate all the peas but one. "The winner!" he said to himself. But even he didn't say who the winner had turned out to be.

# Chapter 5

• • • • • • • • • • • •

"Arthur?"

*Arthur was lying on a mountain of mattresses. Everything was soft and warm and comfortable.*

"Arthur?"

*Arthur poked his head out from beneath the blanket. No one was there. Contentedly, he snuggled in again.*

"ARTHUR!"

*The mattresses abruptly collapsed into one another. Down-down-down-down-down. As they hit the floor, Arthur's eyes shot open.*

His mother was standing over his bed.

"Arthur, you have to get up."

Arthur blinked. "Huh?"

"You have to get up now."

Arthur looked at his alarm clock. "It's only seven-thirty — on a Saturday."

"I know." Mrs. Read smiled. "But Sue Ellen is waiting for you downstairs."

Arthur bolted up. "HERE? NOW?"

His mother nodded. "She said something about a training schedule."

Arthur groaned. He remembered Sue Ellen talking about this the day before, but he hadn't really been paying attention. He hurriedly pulled on some clothes and went down the stairs.

Sue Ellen was waiting in the living room. "It's about time, Arthur," she said. "Gee, you look all rumpled, like you just rolled out of bed."

"There's a good reason for that."

"Well, we don't have time for it now. We're already running behind — or not running, if you see what I mean."

Arthur quickly had some toast and orange juice. Then Sue Ellen pushed him out the door.

"So where should we run?" he asked.

Sue Ellen shook her head. "We can't just run, Arthur. Not like that."

"We can't?" Arthur looked confused.

"No, we have to warm up first. We have to stretch out our muscles so that we won't pull any of them from going too fast."

Arthur yawned. "I don't think that will be a problem."

"Muscles are funny things, Arthur. We have to do this properly. Now let's get started."

She led Arthur through a long stretching routine and then several minutes of running in place.

"All right," said Sue Ellen, "now we're warmed up. Where do you want to run?"

Arthur was breathing heavily. "Nowhere," he muttered, falling down in the grass.

"Come on, Arthur. When the going gets tough, the tough get going."

"Well, that leaves me out."

"Not this time," Sue Ellen said. She helped Arthur up. "Let's head for the park. It'll just be a slow jog."

By the time they reached the park, Arthur was looking for an ambulance. But instead of flashing lights, he spotted Fern and Binky.

"This way," he sputtered to Sue Ellen, running toward them.

Fern was sitting under a tree, reading. Binky was doing push-ups next to her.

"Hi," said Arthur. "What's that? You'd like us to sit down? Great." He dropped like a chopped tree.

"What are you two doing?" asked Sue Ellen.

Binky sat up. "We're practicing for the race."

"Both of you?" asked Sue Ellen.

"Well, I'm doing push-ups," said Binky. "And Fern is keeping track of how many I've done. Right, Fern?"

Fern looked up from her book. "Did you say something?"

Sue Ellen snorted. "Fern, you have to take this seriously."

"I do?"

"This isn't like gym class," said Sue Ellen. "A lot of people will be watching the race. You want to look good out there."

Fern hadn't thought of that. "You really think it's important?"

Sue Ellen nodded.

"All right," said Fern. "Where do I start?"

# Chapter 6

● ● ● ● ● ● ● ● ● ● ●

Two days later Fern dragged herself to the library. Every muscle in her body ached from exercising all the time with Sue Ellen, Binky, and Arthur. Still, she was looking forward to checking out some new mysteries Ms. Turner had mentioned.

But she never reached the shelves. Just inside the front door, she almost collided with the Brain, who was carrying a tall pile of books.

Fern looked at some of the titles. "*Is Your Cardio System Playing with a Full Deck? Electrolytes at the End of the Tunnel.* Um, they sound very interesting."

"And informative," said the Brain. "To win the race, you need a strong scientific background."

Fern yawned.

"What's the matter?" asked the Brain. "You look tired."

"I am. Sue Ellen and Arthur have been running me ragged. Run here, run there, stretch this, stretch that." She shuddered. "Binky seems to like it, though."

The Brain nodded sympathetically. "Their dedication is noteworthy, but their efforts are focused in the wrong direction. Come with me."

"Where?" asked Fern.

"To Muffy's," answered the Brain.

"But I was going to —"

"I'm surprised at you, Fern. I would think that someone who likes to read as much as you do would care more. I mean, don't forget, this is a race for literacy. Don't you want to do your best?"

Fern just sighed.

When the Brain and Fern got to Muffy's, they found her arranging supplies on a shelf.

"We've set up a temporary laboratory," the Brain explained. "We don't have everything yet."

"Like those electrodes they tape to your forehead," said Muffy. "They come in designer colors, but they're on back order."

"We have a lot to analyze," the Brain went on. "Proper running technique involves many factors. There are questions of weight distribution, air displacement, and cardiovascular readiness."

"What does all that mean?" asked Fern.

"It means," said Muffy, "that you have to be prepared. You can't just show up at a race and see what happens. You have to plan; you have to figure things out."

"Exactly," said the Brain. "Now, Fern,

we've done a study of your running style."

"You have?"

The Brain nodded and pulled out a bunch of charts. "We did one of everyone. It's important to know your competition. But in the interests of science, we're willing to share our results." He flipped a couple of pages. "As this chart clearly shows, your toe placement is inefficient."

"It is?"

"Definitely." The Brain explained that she needed to rock her feet more as she stepped down instead of pressing in so hard with her toe.

"Also," he added, "based on your apparent energy level, I believe your endorphins are not generated quickly enough."

"Endorphins?"

"It's stuff your brain makes when you exercise," Muffy explained. "Sounds a bit icky to me. I like things I can see better."

She held out a balloon. "Here, breathe into this. We're going to measure your lung capacity."

Fern backed away toward the door. "Thanks, maybe another time. I really do have to go."

And before they could think of an objection, she took her lung capacity and her toe placement and left as fast as she could.

# Chapter 7

● ● ● ● ● ● ● ● ● ● ●

As Fern made her escape from Muffy's house, she felt a little dizzy. Why did running this race have to be so complicated? All she wanted to do was support a good cause.

She was glad to see Francine and Buster coming down the street. They didn't seem to be exercising or making super-energy potions.

"Hi, Francine. Hi, Buster," said Fern.

Her two friends stopped short.

"Have we met?" said Francine.

"Um, I think you've mistaken us for someone else," said Buster.

"I don't think so," said Fern.

Francine sighed. "Never mind, Buster," she said, removing her sunglasses. "Fern definitely recognized us."

Buster did the same. "That isn't good," he said.

Fern looked confused. "Why not?"

"We were testing these out," Francine explained. "To see how much they would disguise us."

"But you're still wearing your regular clothes," Fern pointed out.

"Ahhhh," said Francine. She and Buster each pulled out a notebook and began writing.

"New wardrobe," said Francine.

"Check," said Buster.

"But not too fancy," Francine added. "We want to blend in."

"Double check," said Buster.

"I'm a little confused," said Fern. "Why do you want disguises?"

"Because of the literacy race," said Francine. "Buster and I expect one of us to win. After that, naturally, we'll be famous."

"Remember when I was a Cat Saver?" said Buster. "We figure this will be ten times bigger than that. It will be hard to go to the mall or a restaurant."

Francine nodded. "We'll have to deal with screaming fans and tons of reporters. And you know how tiring that can get after a few months. So we thought we should practice ways we could still go out in public."

"I see," said Fern. "Is that all?"

"Oh, no," said Francine. "There's lots more to worry about. We have to decide which talk shows to go on."

"And which products to endorse," said Buster. "I'm hoping for an ice-cream company. That way I'll get free samples."

"Can you believe him?" Francine said to Fern.

"It is a little hard," Fern admitted.

"Absolutely," said Francine. "There's no future in ice cream. Now, sports equipment, that's another story."

Fern sighed.

"Have you thought about this at all?" Francine asked.

"Can't say that I have," said Fern.

"That's a mistake. I mean, even if you don't win this time, there will be other races. And you don't want to wait until it's too late. When the crowd and the reporters are surrounding you . . ."

"Don't forget the flashing lights," said Buster. "All those photographers . . ."

Francine nodded. "At that point it's hard to think clearly. And you certainly don't want to look stupid on national television."

Fern paled. "No, no, I wouldn't want that."

"Why don't you practice with us?"

41

asked Buster. "We need someone to play the adoring fan."

"That's very tempting," said Fern. "But I know I have something else to do somewhere."

"Okay," said Francine. "But keep in mind what we said."

"Don't worry," said Fern. "I couldn't forget if I tried."

# Chapter 8

● ● ● ● ● ● ● ● ● ● ● ●

"Only one day to go till the race," said Arthur.

He was standing at the school bike rack with Sue Ellen, Binky, Muffy, the Brain, Francine, and Buster.

"That means only a light routine today," said Sue Ellen.

Arthur sighed. "I think my muscles are beginning to get muscles," he said.

"We're ready," said the Brain. "Muffy and I have worked everything out down to the last micrometer."

"And I've got eighteen sponsors," said Muffy. "We'll raise tons of money."

"I have a bunch of sponsors, too," said Buster. "It helps when your mom works for a newspaper. The people there really care about reading."

"My dad got some of the businesses on his trash route to back me," said Francine. "They won't be disappointed."

"My parents are going to sell home-made desserts to the crowd," said Arthur. "And all the profits will be donated."

Binky licked his lips. "I hope they save something sweet for me."

"Hey, Binky," said Francine, "where's Fern, anyway?"

Binky shrugged. "Beats me. She told me she had done enough."

"Not with us," said Arthur and Sue Ellen.

"Or us," said Muffy and the Brain.

"We've barely seen her," said Francine.

"Hey, there she is!" said Buster, waving.

They all turned to see Fern approaching

in the distance. But once she saw them staring and waving at her, she turned away.

"Poor Fern," said Buster.

"She must be so worried," Francine said.

"I wish we could help. But we tried," said the Brain.

When Fern had seen everyone looking at her, she had suddenly decided to go to the library. She didn't want to hear any more race strategies or running techniques or anything else.

She found a quiet corner and opened a book, trying to read. But it was hard to concentrate, and she could feel herself getting sleepy.

*Fern was strapped to a treadmill, forced to run as fast as the belt beneath her feet was going.*

*"I need to rest," she said.*

*"Nonsense," said Sue Ellen, who was regu-*

lating the treadmill controls. "We haven't begun to test your limits."

The Brain appeared behind her, holding a cup filled with some bubbling liquid.

"What's that?" asked Fern.

"My new Proton Energy Drink. It will give you added strength and endurance."

"No thanks," said Fern.

"But you have to drink," said Francine, leading over a group of reporters and photographers. "Otherwise, you'll never be famous."

"I don't want to be famous!" Fern insisted.

"You see," Francine said to the press. "I told you she was modest."

The photographers began snapping pictures, and the flashing bulbs left spots in front of Fern's eyes.

"Let me go!" she shouted. "I just want to be myself."

"Fern?"

Fern opened her eyes.

Ms. Turner was standing in front of her. "We'll be closing in a few minutes."

"Oh, thanks," said Fern.

Ms. Turner smiled. "Catching up on your rest before the big race tomorrow? You must be really excited."

Fern sighed and gathered up her things. She felt nervous, tired, awkward, and uncomfortable. *Excited* didn't make her list at all.

# Chapter 9

On the day of the big race, the school grounds were decorated with balloons and crepe paper. A big banner reading LAKEWOOD FOR LITERACY stood over the starting line. Everyone was warming up around it.

The principal, Mr. Haney, spoke into a microphone. "May I have your attention, please?" he asked. "The fifth grade will start first. The fourth grade will leave five minutes later, and so on. Now I want everyone to take a deep breath. Remember, we're here to have fun, get some exercise, and raise money for a good cause."

Arthur and his friends gathered with the other third-graders.

"Are you ready, Fern?" asked Sue Ellen.

"I guess," said Fern, who was standing with Binky.

Sue Ellen jogged in place. "Arthur's ready. Aren't you, Arthur?"

"Are there doctors here?" he asked. "Is there an ambulance close by? What if I need oxygen?"

"It's interesting," said the Brain, "that while the air we breathe is almost three-quarters nitrogen, it's oxygen we get in an emergency."

"Don't worry, Fern," said Muffy. "Just remember everything we told you, and you'll be fine."

"I'm okay, Muffy. Honest."

"Of course you are," said Francine. "Buster and I gave you all the tips you'll need to make the race a success."

Binky started counting on his fingers.

"What are you doing?" Fern asked.

"Just trying to keep track of everything," he said.

Once the fifth- and fourth-graders had left, the third-graders approached the starting line.

"Ready?" cried Mr. Haney. "Set. Go!"

He blew on his whistle.

The third-graders surged forward. They were bunched together at first, but soon spread out along the route. Sue Ellen and Arthur were in front of the pack.

"Faster, Arthur!" gasped Sue Ellen. "We need to keep our lead."

Arthur nodded — and tried to keep up. But Sue Ellen's pace was too much for him.

"I have to stop," he wheezed. "I have an ache in my side."

"It's all in your mind," she said. "You just have to . . . oh!" Suddenly, her side ached, too.

As they slowed to a walk, Muffy and the Brain passed them.

"Your strides are too long," the Brain told her.

"They are not," said Muffy. "They're just right."

The Brain shook his head. "You're in great danger of severely bruising your instep."

"You're making that up."

The Brain frowned. "I don't make things up. Come on over here, and I'll show you." He led her to the side of the road.

As the Brain knelt down beside Muffy, Francine and Buster surged past.

"Hooray, Francine!" said a voice in the crowd.

"Go, Buster!" shouted another.

They both smiled. "This is it," Francine said. "It's our big moment."

"Francine, where are you going?" asked Buster.

"These are our fans, Buster. They want to congratulate us."

"Oh, of course," said Buster, running over to join her.

Francine and Buster left the course to take their bows, and Fern and Binky passed them.

"Uh-oh!" said Binky.

"What's the matter?" asked Fern.

"I forget what I'm supposed to do next."

"Just keep running," said Fern.

Binky shook his head and stopped.

"What are you doing?" asked Fern.

"I can't run and think at the same time. You go on ahead."

Fern shrugged. "Okay," she said, and she left Binky behind, scratching his head.

Fern was all by herself now. She had to admit it felt good to stretch her legs and feel the wind in her hair. She wondered if Phidippides had felt this way running from Marathon.

As Fern approached the end, the cheering on the sidelines grew louder and louder. Everyone was smiling and waving at her. She smiled and waved back.

And then she crossed the finish line.

# Chapter 10

• • • • • • • • • • • •

All of the winners were standing with Mr. Haney. "I want to thank everyone for participating in Lakewood for Literacy. We met our financial goal, which we could never have done without everyone's help," the principal said.

The crowd cheered.

As the winners gathered in front of him, Mr. Haney began handing out the prizes.

"And for the third grade," he said, "congratulations, Fern!" He handed her a book of poems.

"Way to go!" shouted Buster.

"I can't believe it," said Francine. "We should ask for a recount."

"There's no recount," said the Brain. "This was a race, not an election."

"I didn't see Fern worrying about her instep," Muffy reminded him.

"Fern didn't worry about anything," said Arthur. "It was kind of like that old story. We were all hares. And Fern was the tortoise."

When the ceremony was over, Fern came over to show them her prize.

Sue Ellen looked through the pages. "It's beautiful. So, now that you've won, Fern, what next?"

"Gee, I don't know exactly."

"Don't worry," said Francine. "We can give you advice."

"We have plenty," added the Brain.

Fern smiled. "That's for sure," she said.